DISNEY
PIRATES of the CARIBBEAN

This Pirates of the Caribbean
Annual belongs to:

Captain ....
Scribble your pirate name here!

EGMONT
We bring stories to life

Based on the screenplay written by Ted Elliot & Terry Rossio
Based on characters created by Ted Elliot & Terry Rossio and Stuart Beattie and Jay Wolpert
Based on Walt Disney's Pirates of the Caribbean
Produced by Jerry Bruckheimer
Directed by Gore Verbinski

First published in Great Britain in 2007 by Egmont UK Limited
239 Kensington High Street, London W8 6SA
ISBN 978 1 4052 3183 1
3 5 7 9 10 8 6 4 2
Printed in Italy
Written and edited by Jo Strange
Designed by Colin Treanor

DISNEYPIRATES.COM

Welcome to your official

Disney
PIRATES of the CARIBBEAN

ANNUAL 2008

LISTEN UP, galley-rats!
If you're a wannabe swashbucklin'
pirate then you've come to the
right place! These 'ere pages are
packed with facts, tales and all the
secrets of the Seven Seas.
If your stomach is strong,
CLIMB ABOARD!

Contents

Welcome to

Think you know Jack Sparrow from Jack the Monkey? Here's your guide to some of the faces you'll meet in the Caribbean seas ...

Barbossa

Bootstrap Bill

Tia brought Barbossa back from the dead

Jack and Tia are old friends

Tia Dalma

Bootstrap must serve Davy for an eternity

Will is Bootstrap Bill's son

Will Turner

Tia and Davy own matching pendants

Davy Jones

Will needs to stab Davy's heart to free his father

Will bartered the maps to World's End from Sao Feng

Elizabeth is engaged to be married to Will

Sao Feng

Elizabeth captained Sao Feng's ship

Elizabeth Swann

Governor Swann is Elizabeth's father

the Caribbean

Barbossa led Jack's crew to mutiny

Pintel and Ragetti are members of Jack's crew

Gibbs is Jack's loyal first mate

Jack Sparrow

Pintel & Ragetti

Jack owes a blood debt to Davy

Beckett wants Jack to be his privateer

Joshamee Gibbs

Gibbs once served in the Navy under Norrington

Beckett possesses Davy Jones' heart

Jack is Norrington's nemesis!

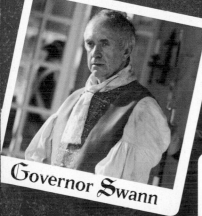

Governor Swann

Governor Swann serves Beckett

Lord Cutler Beckett

Beckett promoted Norrington to Admiral

James Norrington

Pirate

Life on the Caribbean seas can be dangerous but land offers little safety! On which of these pirate stop-offs would you prefer to find yourself?

Port Royal

This busy town on the coast of Jamaica was founded by the English. It is ruled by Governor Swann, Elizabeth Swann's father. Dominating Port Royal's harbour is Fort Charles, a large government building that houses the prison.

PORT ROYAL

TORTUGA

Tortuga

The island of Tortuga is a true pirate haven. Lying to the north of Hispaniola, it was named by the Spanish because of its turtle-like shape. Vibrant and dangerous, there is never a dull moment in the town's rum-drenched taverns. Jack Sparrow is no stranger here!

Rumrunner's Isle

Once a rum-smuggling hideout, this island has long been deserted. Jack has been marooned here not once, but twice, the first time with nothing but a pistol and one shot for company. Jack claims he escaped on the backs of two sea turtles!

RUMRUNNER'S ISLE

Places

Isla De Muerta

Isla de Muerta means "Island of Death"! Within its creepy caves, the chest containing Cortes' Aztec Gold was discovered. It is said that the island cannot be found – except by those who know where it is!

ISLA DE MUERTA

ISLA DE PELEGOSTOS

Isla De Pelegostos

This green, mountainous island is home to a tribe of flesh-eating natives called the Pelegostos. Brutal and savage, they hunt in packs, looking for their next meal.

Isla Cruces

Isla Cruces is the island where Davy Jones' chest was buried. Once a bustling island, it now lies abandoned. Its name means "Crosses Island", perhaps because of the many gravestones found in the grounds of the ruined church.

ISLA CRUCES

The Bayou

The eerie forest along the Pantano River is a scary place to be. Faces look out at you from behind trees and the mysterious mist gives it a haunting chill. It is by entering the Bayou that you'll come to find Tia Dalma's shack.

THE BAYOU

The Curse of the Black Pearl

1   Elizabeth first met Will Turner when she was just a girl aboard her father's ship, the *HMS Dauntless*. She'd spotted Will in the ocean and he was hauled on deck. Afraid he'd be mistaken for a pirate, Elizabeth took the gold Medallion she'd found around Will's neck.

2   Eight years later and alone in her room in Port Royal's mansion house, Elizabeth put on the Medallion.

Meanwhile, a man wearing a battered leather hat stepped off a fast-sinking trawler into Port Royal harbour. Two guards asked him his business.

"It is my intention to commandeer one of those ships, pick up a crew in Tortuga, raid, pillage, plunder and otherwise pilfer my weasly guts out!" said the man.

3   Later that day, the newly promoted Commodore James Norrington asked Elizabeth to marry him. The bodice of her new dress was so tight that, before she could answer, Elizabeth fainted and fell off the cliff edge into the sea!

The man in the hat saw Elizabeth fall and rescued her.

4   "Well, well," said Norrington, sternly, as he shook the man's hand. "Jack Sparrow, isn't it?"

"Captain Jack Sparrow, if you please, sir," replied Jack.

Jack Sparrow was a wanted pirate. After an impressive escape and a swordfight with Will Turner, Captain Jack was recaptured and taken to Fort Charles prison, sentenced to death.

5   That night, Port Royal was raided by pirates. They were looking for something – and Elizabeth had it.

"Parlay!" cried Elizabeth, when pirates cornered her. "Parlay" was part of the Pirate Code and it meant the pirates couldn't harm her. Instead, they took her to their captain.

Aboard the *Black Pearl*, Elizabeth faced Captain Barbossa. Sensing her Medallion was important to him, she threatened to drop it into the sea unless they stopped the raid.

"You have a name, missy?" asked Barbossa.

"Elizabeth ... Turner," she replied. The pirates' eyes lit up. They left the town, taking Elizabeth with them.

That night, Elizabeth watched in horror as the crew turned into terrifying skeletons in the moonlight. Their greed for Cortes' Aztec Gold had cost them, for every crew member was now cursed and undead.

6   Will cared deeply for Elizabeth and was determined to rescue her. He offered to help Jack escape from prison if Jack helped him find the *Black Pearl*. Jack agreed and Will forced open the door to Jack's cell. The pair set out to sea, "commandeering" the Navy's *HMS Interceptor*.

In Tortuga, they assembled a crew and set off to find the *Black Pearl*. With the help of his compass, Jack knew just where it would be.

7 In the caves on Isla de Muerta, the cursed pirates surrounded their mountain of stolen treasure, topped with a chest containing the Aztec Gold. Finally, they had what they needed – all eight hundred and eighty-two pieces of Cortes' gold and the blood of a Turner. The pirates took a pin-prick of Elizabeth's blood and dropped the Medallion into the chest. Seconds passed but nothing happened. The curse hadn't lifted. Barbossa realised Elizabeth had lied about her surname and hers wasn't the blood they needed.

8 Jack Sparrow knew whose blood Barbossa needed.

Arriving in the caves, Will rescued Elizabeth and took her to the *Interceptor*. Meanwhile, Jack struck a deal with Barbossa. Jack would lead Barbossa to the person he needed if Barbossa gave him back the *Black Pearl*.

Before long, Barbossa caught up with and attacked the *Interceptor*, taking Elizabeth and the crew captive. Now it was Will's turn to make a deal.

9 Will told Barbossa that he was the son of Bootstrap Bill Turner and that unless Barbossa did as he said, he'd jump overboard — leaving Barbossa cursed forever.

"Name your terms," hissed Barbossa.

"Elizabeth goes free. And Jack," Will demanded, but his plan backfired because he didn't say when or where. Barbossa forced Jack and Elizabeth to walk the plank, while Will remained captive.

Jack and Elizabeth swam to Rumrunner's Isle and, for the second time, Jack was forced to watch Barbossa sail off with his ship!

10 The next morning, the naval crew of the *HMS Dauntless* was out looking for Elizabeth. They soon spotted her smoke signals.

Once safe, Elizabeth pleaded with her father to help her save Will, but he refused. She turned to Norrington, asking him to save Will as a wedding gift for her. Then Jack was ordered to lead them to Isla de Muerta.

As the *Dauntless* neared the island caves, Jack persuaded Norrington to let him enter alone, to draw out the pirates. Norrington didn't know that the pirates were undead and couldn't be killed!

11 Inside the caves, Jack arrived just as Barbossa was about to kill Will.

"You don't want to be doing that, mate," said Jack to Barbossa. The Navy was waiting outside and Barbossa's crew would have no chance of surviving an attack if they were mortal again. Barbossa sent his men to fight the Navy in their skeletal form and Will's life was spared ... for the moment.

12 Barbossa was angry and soon a fierce fight broke out. Jack, having picked up a piece of the Aztec Gold, also turned into a skeleton.

"That's interesting," he said, examining his fleshless frame.

13 Jack quickly tossed a piece of Aztec Gold to Will. Barbossa aimed his pistol at Elizabeth, but it was too late to bargain ... Jack had shot him.

"Ten years you carry that pistol and now you waste your shot," snarled Barbossa.

"He didn't waste it," said Will, dropping the gold into the chest. The curse lifted. Barbossa suddenly came back to life, only to die from the gunshot, seconds later.

14 Outside, the now mortal pirates surrendered to the Navy. As Will rowed Jack and Elizabeth out of the cave, they saw the *Black Pearl* sail off into the distance. Jack had hoped to escape on the *Pearl* but his crew had stuck to the Pirate Code and left without him.

"They've done what's right by them. Can't expect more than that," sighed Jack.

Aboard the *Dauntless*, Jack was captured by the Navy.

15 Some time later in Port Royal, a crowd gathered to see Jack Sparrow being hanged.

"This is wrong," whispered Elizabeth to her father.

Suddenly, a man wearing a large hat made his way through the crowd – it was Will Turner. He calmly told Elizabeth that he loved her and then used his brilliant sword skills to free Jack from the noose. Jack and Will tried hard to escape but were soon surrounded.

16 "You forget your place, Turner" said Norrington.

"It's right here," Will replied, "between you and Jack."

"As is mine," added Elizabeth, joining them.

The officers lowered their weapons. As Jack stepped backwards, he tipped off the edge of the cliff and into the sea. Waiting for him was the *Black Pearl* and his crew. "Now ... bring me that horizon," said Jack, taking the helm.

Jack Sparrow is the Caribbean's most notorious pirate. And that's *Captain* Jack Sparrow to you ... savvy?

Name: Jack Sparrow

Ships: The *Jolly Mon*, *HMS Interceptor* ("borrowed" from the Navy), the *Black Pearl*

Personality: Deceptively smart, able to outwit anyone he meets

Weapons: Sword, pistol

Skills: Expert swordfighter, a smooth talker

Prized possessions: Compass, hat, pistol, sword

Young Jack

Little is known about Jack's past, although it is thought he was once a merchant marine. This is perhaps where he learned his first-rate swordfighting skills.

Jack's most guarded possession is his compass. Instead of pointing north, it points to what the holder wants most. Jack bartered the compass from Tia Dalma.

Jack Sparrow

Jack's tricorn hat is very important to him. Despite all the scrapes he gets in, he always manages to keep hold of it.

Jack isn't the finest pistoleer in the Caribbean. However, his razor-sharp mind always gets him out of trouble.

" Is this a **dream?** I thought not. If it were, **there'd be rum"**

– *Jack Sparrow*

Black

Often simply referred to as the *Pearl*, this feared pirate ship can out-sail any other on the Seven Seas.

Blackened

The *Black Pearl* has been Jack Sparrow's ship for many years. Under Jack's captaincy, Cutler Beckett hired the ship to transport cargo from Africa. Jack learned the "cargo" was slaves and so he set them free. Furious, Beckett found Jack, and burned and sank his ship. Some time later, Jack made a pact with Davy Jones to raise the ship and captain her for thirteen years. Jack named his blackened ship, the *Black Pearl*.

Don't be fooled by the *Black Pearl*'s ragged, threadbare sails. There is something special about this ship. It is said she rides on a supernatural wind ...

Dark as the Night

The *Black Pearl*'s striking black hull and sails make her look very intimidating to oncoming ships. During the night, the *Pearl* is barely visible, especially when the crew puts out the deck lamps.

20

Pearl Crew

Pearls are said to symbolise magic and purity. Black pearls are found in the Tahiti islands in the South Pacific.

Joshamee Gibbs

Jack's superstitious first mate is happy so long as there is rum. Gibbs completely trusts Jack, even though he sometimes acts a little strangely!

Cotton

A mute old seadog, this deckhand's thoughts are voiced through his ever-present parrot.

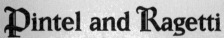

Pintel and Ragetti

These dimwitted fools are often more of a hindrance than a help on board Jack's ship!

Ruthless and underhand, this experienced pirate captain doesn't suffer fools gladly ...

Name: Barbossa

Ships: *Black Pearl*

Personality: Commanding, confident and cunning in equal measure

Skills: Strategic sailor and legendary swordsman

Prized possessions: Flintock gun, ring showing a lion's head

Notes of interest: Barbossa's real name is not known

Jack's First Mate?

Barbossa once reported to Jack aboard the *Black Pearl*. However, Barbossa betrayed Jack, leading the crew to mutiny and becoming its cursed captain. Jack eventually got his revenge, killing Barbossa on Isla de Muerta.

Through methods unknown, powerful mystic, Tia Dalma, resurrected Barbossa from the dead.

He may be older than most pirates, but Barbossa's swordfighting skills are famous. Few question his authority when under his command.

Barbossa's most loyal friend is "Jack the Monkey". Barbossa named him after Captain Jack Sparrow.

66 You'd best start believing in **ghost stories,** Miss Turner . . . you're in one.**99**

– *Captain Barbossa*

Captain Barbossa

Pirate

Pirates rarely obey the law, but they still like to live by a few rules!

Captain's Orders

Like naval ships, every pirate ship has a captain, to give the orders and decide on the course of action. Unlike naval crews, however, pirate crews are more democratic. A "Pirate Code" was drawn up to ensure each crew member has his say and receives his fair share of booty.

"The Code is more what you would call guidelines than actual rules."

– Captain Barbossa

"The Code? You're pirates! Hang the Code!"

– Elizabeth Swann

Keep to the Code

The original, handwritten Pirate Code was the work of pirates Morgan and Bartholomew. It is kept by Captain Teague, Jack Sparrow's father.

Code

Introduction to the Pirate Code

These Artycles of Agreement, being a Concorde of lyke-mynded Marauders, Thieves, Cutthroats and Scoundrels, hear-bye shalle serve as the bynding ~~rules~~ guidelines for the Proper Behayvior and Con-duct of our Sea-faring lyves, brief and cruel as they maye be, so say on this date the Pirate Lords of the Brethren Court, and to all who affix their names to This Code, know that by it ye must Abide or Perish.

These plankes we laye downe for our Villainous Creed,
Of Pylfering Plunder from all Shippes at sea,
Add your Marks here only if hard-bound ye be,
To hold fast to this Code, a Pyrate's Lyfe to leade.

A Pirate's Right

A pirate under attack can make his enemy call a truce by saying the word "parlay". The enemy must hold fire while a deal is struck. Be warned: the protection of parlay is only temporary!

Pirate

What is the first rule of being a pirate? Never trust a fellow pirate!

Jack's Trickster Traits
Jack Sparrow ...

... wears flamboyant costumes to distract the eyes of an enemy.

... tells long, complicated stories that cleverly mix lies with elements of truth, leaving his audience completely confused!

... sometimes acts the fool in order to disarm opponents and catch them by surprise.

... notices things that most other people don't – and acts on it quickly!

Master Trickster

Jack Sparrow is the finest trickster the Caribbean has ever seen. No one can get out of scrapes in such style as Jack, and only he would be brave or crazy enough to steal a ship from under the Navy's nose! Being a true pirate, Jack would never call this stealing. He prefers the term, "borrowing".

Trickery

66 A dishonest man can always be trusted to be dishonest. It's the **honest** ones you can't predict. 99
— *Jack Sparrow*

Life on

If you think a pirate's life's for you, here are a few things you'll need to know ...

Pirate Speak

Pirates like to make up their own words. Practise saying those below in your best pirate accent!

Ahoy – Hello

Aye! – Why, yes!

Avast! – Stop and pay attention!

Pieces of eight – A silver coin, cut into eight pieces

Grog – A pirate's favourite liquor

Sea dog – An experienced sailor

Booty – Loot or treasure

Landlubber – An insult, someone not used to being aboard a ship!

Know Your Knots

Tying knots is an essential part of a pirate's life. Grab a length of string and have a go at tying the knots below.

figure of eight knot

reef knot

sailor's knot

granny knot

Can you tell the difference between a granny knot and a reef knot?

Board

Flag Facts

Every pirate captain worth his booty has a skull and crossbones flag flying from the mizzenmast of his ship.

The Skull and Crossbones flag is known as the Jolly Roger. This comes from the French, "Joli Rouge", meaning "pretty red".

Some pirate flags were dyed red to suggest they had been dipped in the blood of those who dared to challenge them!

If the Jolly Roger flag is raised upside down, it means there won't just be death, there will be torture, too!

There's pirate in young Will Turner's blood, as his ancestry begins to show in his actions ...

Name: Will Turner

Personality: Determined and courageous, prepared to take risks

Skills: Excellent at making swords – and using them

Prized possessions: The knife given to him by his father

Notes of interest: Will Turner made the ceremonial sword awarded to James Norrington

Long Lost Father

As a child, Will believed his father was a merchant marine. After his mother's death, Will travelled to the Caribbean to search for him. It wasn't until Will met Jack Sparrow that he learned his father was a famous pirate, Bootstrap Bill Turner.

Bootstrap Bill

Will is a master swordsman, thanks to continuous practice in R. Brown's blacksmiths where he worked as an apprentice.

When Will first met Tia Dalma, she instinctively knew his name and said he had "a touch of destiny" about him.

Will can be extremely brave when he needs to. Aboard the *Flying Dutchman* he dared to play a game of Liar's Dice with the ship's captain!

Will Turner

"I challenge **Davy Jones!**"
— *Will Turner*

Enchanted by pirate tales as a young girl, brave Elizabeth Swann possesses many pirate qualities herself ...

Name: Elizabeth Swann

Personality: Adventurous and spirited, refuses to play the traditional role of a governor's daughter

Ship: *Empress*

Skills: Good at improvising and using disguises

Weapons: Sword, pistol

Notes of interest: Was prepared to marry James Norrington to save Will Turner's life

A Free Spirit

As the child of a governor, young Elizabeth Swann was forced to follow society's rules. She longed for freedom and escaped the boredom of Port Royal's mansion house by reading books about the exciting lives of pirates.

It was Joshamee Gibbs, Jack Sparrow's loyal friend, who told pirate tales to Elizabeth, when he was still a member of the British Navy.

Elizabeth is more comfortable wearing pirate clothes than in the fine dresses her father buys her.

Like some of the pirates she's met, Elizabeth has a ruthless streak. She ensured the Kraken got who it came for by chaining Jack Sparrow to his ship and now she's set to become a Pirate Lord herself.

Elizabeth Swann

"You like pain?
Try wearing a corset!**"**

– Elizabeth Swann

For James Norrington, honour and reputation is everything. Pirates have stood in his way for too long!

Name: James Norrington

Rank: Admiral

Personality: Determined, formal and respectful – even to his foes

Ships: *HMS Interceptor*, *HMS Dauntless*

Skills: Norrington is a trained military leader, swordsman and sailor

Weapons: Sword, pistol

Pursuit of Pirates

This proud officer's determination to capture Jack Sparrow became so intense that he wrecked his ship in a hurricane trying to catch him. Norrington was discharged from the Navy for his foolishness. He managed to regain his reputation and now works under Lord Cutler Beckett's command.

Norrington has learned to mask his true feelings in order to have an air of authority – a trait that Elizabeth Swann cannot bear!

Norrington stole the Letters of Marque from Jack. He wrote his name on them to ensure he was spared the death penalty.

Norrington uses what some might call "pirate methods" to get what he wants. He delivered Davy Jones' heart to Cutler Beckett and was promoted to Admiral.

James Norrington

"Do excuse me while I kill the man that ruined my life."

– James Norrington

Dead Man's Chest

1 On what should have been their wedding day, Elizabeth Swann and Will Turner were arrested and sentenced to death for conspiring to set free a convicted pirate.

2 Lord Cutler Beckett, senior officer of the East India Trading Company, summoned Will to his office.

"By your efforts, Jack Sparrow was set free. I would like you to go to him and recover a certain property in his possession," said Beckett.

Will had no choice but to agree.

Later, Elizabeth also paid Beckett a visit. Holding a pistol to his head, she made him sign the Letters of Marque to secure Will's freedom. During their negotiations, Elizabeth learned that Beckett sought a chest.

Jack Sparrow wanted the very same chest. After escaping from a Turkish prison, he boarded his beloved *Black Pearl* with his first clue towards finding the chest — a drawing of a key.

3   That night, Jack got a visit from Bootstrap Bill, Will's father and a member of the *Flying Dutchman's* barnacle-encrusted crew. Bootstrap reminded Jack of the blood debt he owed Davy Jones. Either Jack served one hundred years aboard Davy's ship, or he faced being dragged to the ocean depths by the Kraken, Davy's terrifying sea monster.

As Bootstrap disappeared, the Black Spot appeared in Jack's palm. This meant that the Kraken was after him. Petrified, Jack ordered his crew to head for land.

4   Unfortunately, the nearest land was home to a huge tribe of flesh-eating savages.

Finding the *Black Pearl* beached on the shore, Will went inland to look for Jack. He was soon caught and brought to the tribe's chief – who turned out to be Jack Sparrow!

The tribe believed Jack was a god trapped in human form. They intended to roast him on a spit, but Jack narrowly escaped. Jack, Will and the crew reached the safety of the *Black Pearl* and set off, keeping to shallow waters.

5   "I need that compass, Jack," said Will, hoping to quickly get what Beckett wanted. "I must trade it for Elizabeth's freedom."

"I shall trade you the compass, if you will help me ... to find this," replied Jack, showing Will his drawing of a key. Jack and Will had a deal.

6 Soon, on the banks of the eerie Pantano river, the crew entered Tia Dalma's shack. Tia was an old friend of Jack's and a powerful mystic.

Inside, the crew learned the legendary tale of Davy Jones' lost love. He'd ripped out his still-beating heart and locked it away in a chest. The key Jack wanted unlocked the chest.

Seeing the Black Spot on Jack's palm, Tia gave him a jar of dirt.

"Land is where you are safe, Jack Sparrow. And so you will carry land with you," she said.

7 "Douse the lamps," said Jack, as Will rowed out to the *Flying Dutchman* in the darkness. Will knew very little about Davy Jones, but his ignorance was short-lived.

"What is your purpose here?" boomed Davy, a terrifying half-man, half-sea-creature.

"Jack Sparrow sent me to settle his debt," mumbled Will, nervously.

Sensing Jack was close, Davy tracked him down and set him a challenge. Davy gave Jack three days to find one hundred souls to serve aboard his ship. If he succeeded, Jack's soul would be spared.

Davy decided to keep Will as a good faith payment.

8 On the watery, roach-infested decks of the *Flying Dutchman*, Will met his father, Bootstrap Bill, for the first time. Will showed him what he was looking for.

Bootstrap was desperate for Will not to suffer the same fate he had. When Will played a high-stakes game of Liar's Dice with Davy, Bootstrap joined in and lost on purpose. Bootstrap was doomed to serve an eternity aboard the *Flying Dutchman*.

9 But Will had only wanted to find out where Davy kept the key to his chest. That night, as Davy slept, Will stole the key, carefully teasing it out of Davy's beard of tentacles. Just before he escaped, Bootstrap gave Will his knife – his only possession.

"I take this with a promise," said Will. "I'll find a way to sever Jones' hold on you."

10 Meanwhile, in a tavern in Tortuga, Jack's first mate, Joshamee Gibbs, interviewed would-be sailors to hand over to Davy Jones.

"And what's your story?" Gibbs asked the next candidate in the queue.

It was James Norrington. Having lost his commission, he was angrier at Jack than ever and a brawl soon erupted.

Watching it unfold was Elizabeth Swann, who'd disguised herself as a sailor to come in search of Will.

"What has the world done to you?" she sighed, finding Norrington face-down in a pool of mud.

11 All had little choice but to stick together, so Jack, Elizabeth and a reluctant Norrington prepared to set sail from Tortuga. Jack was struggling to find a bearing, so he gave his compass to Elizabeth. Her desperation to find her beloved Will – by finding the chest – would be sure to point them in the direction Jack wanted to go.

12 "This doesn't work," complained Elizabeth, reading Jack's compass. "It certainly doesn't tell you what you want most."

"Yes it does," cried Jack. "You're sitting on it!"

The compass had led them to Isla Cruces. Jack and Norrington started to dig and they soon uncovered a large box. Inside it, was a smaller, heavier chest. They all heard the thumping sound of Davy's heart.

"So, you were telling the truth," said Norrington.

"I do that quite a lot. But people are always surprised," Jack replied.

13 "With good reason," came another voice. It was Will Turner. He was angry at Jack for leaving him with Davy Jones.

Jack, Norrington and Will all wanted the key to the chest for different reasons. A fierce swordfight broke out.

14 During the fight, Elizabeth was left guarding the chest. She thought a swordfight was a silly way to resolve a dispute and was furious with all three of them. She pretended to faint to distract their attention, but it didn't work.

Seeing their chance, Pintel and Ragetti ran off with the chest. Elizabeth chased them into the jungle but soon, she was being chased, too.

15 Realising his key had been stolen by Will Turner, Davy Jones knew his heart wasn't safe. Davy was able to set foot on land only once every ten years, so he sent his grisly crew members on to Isla Cruces to retrieve his chest for him. Terrified, Pintel and Ragetti gave up the chest to Davy's crew.

Nearby, Jack Sparrow had obtained the key, while Will and Norrington continued to fight. Seeing one of Davy's men running off with the chest, Jack threw a coconut at him and knocked his head clean off!

16 Finally alone with the chest, Jack quickly opened it and took the heart. He raced back to the shore towards the longboat.

As Jack's crew fought hard to hold Davy's men back, Norrington spotted the Letters of Marque in the longboat. Mysteriously, Norrington gave Elizabeth, Jack and Will a chance to escape by running back to the island with the chest, distracting Davy's crew.

17 On the open seas, the *Pearl* and the *Dutchman* faced each other. Suddenly, Jack dropped his Jar of Dirt. The heart that he'd hidden there was no longer inside it – Jack had lost his bargaining tool!

Jack's only hope now was to get as far away from Davy Jones as possible.

"Hard to starboard," said Jack, directing his crew to turn the ship.

The *Pearl* out-sailed the *Dutchman*, but Davy Jones had a more powerful form of attack than gunfire ...

18 Knowing the Kraken was about to strike, Jack rowed away, leaving his crew to its fate.

Soon, the Kraken's slimy tentacles climbed the hull of the ship. Under Will's command, the crew gathered its barrels of gunpowder. Elizabeth prepared to shoot at the barrels but Jack returned and took over. Jack's shot made a huge explosion that sent the Kraken underwater.

"Did we kill it?" asked a crew member.

"No, we just made it angry," replied Gibbs. "We're not out of this yet."

19 As the crew crammed into the last remaining longboat, the Kraken came back with all its force.

"It's after you, not the ship," said Elizabeth, leaning close to Jack. As she kissed him, she chained him to the ship's mast and then ran to the longboat to escape.

Jack sensed the Kraken's huge mouth behind him. He turned and was sprayed with its rotten, slimy breath.

"Hello, beastie," said Jack, before leaping into the Kraken's mouth with his sword held high.

20 Some time later, in Port Royal, Lord Cutler Beckett received a visitor. It was James Norrington and he had the Letters of Marque with him, the legal pardon meant for Jack.

"If you intend to claim these, then you must have something to trade," said Beckett. "Do you have the compass?"

"Better," replied Norrington, as he dropped a small bag containing Davy Jones' beating heart on to Beckett's desk.

21 Meanwhile, on the *Flying Dutchman*, Davy was triumphant.

"Jack Sparrow. Our debt is settled," said Davy, smugly, having watched his pet swallow Jack and drag the *Black Pearl* to the ocean floor.

"Open the chest. Open the chest, I need to see it!" Davy demanded of his crew. But as Davy peered into the chest, his face suddenly quivered in despair. His heart had been stolen!

"Curse you, Jack Sparrow!" boomed Davy, in fury.

22 Still distressed by their captain's death, Elizabeth, Will and the remaining members of Jack's crew made their way to Tia Dalma's shack.

Inside, they all toasted to Jack, agreeing that there was no other pirate in the Caribbean quite like him.

Seeing Elizabeth so upset, Will asked Tia Dalma if there was a way they could bring Jack back.

23 "Would you do it? Hmm?" replied Tia. One by one, they all said, "Aye."

"If you're going to brave the weird and haunted shores at World's End, then you will need a captain that knows those waters," she continued.

To the crew's amazement, Captain Barbossa stepped into the room. He was supposed to be dead!

"So, what's become of my ship?" he said, his undead monkey sitting on his shoulder.

The Pelegostos

Isla de Pelegostos is home to a savage tribe called the Pelegostos. If you set foot on their island, beware ... the Pelegostos hunt in packs and carry razor-sharp spears!

Jack the Chief

The Pelegostos believed that Jack Sparrow was a god trapped in human form. To release his spirit, they intended to roast him! Jack being Jack, managed to escape — with the spit still tied to him!

Can you find 6 differences between these two pictures?

The answers can be found on page 69.

Mysterious Animals

Like their pirate owners, pets in the Caribbean are far from normal ...

Cursed Monkey

Jack is Captain Barbossa's undead, mangy monkey. Named after Jack Sparrow, he became cursed after stealing a piece of Aztec Gold. Jack has a nasty habit of jumping out on people to surprise them. He enjoys spying on people, too!

Cotton's Parrot

Nobody knows how, but mute crew member, Cotton, trained his parrot to talk for him. However, it's not always clear whether it's Cotton's thoughts or his own that he's squawking! The parrot doesn't have a name — the crew all call him "Cotton's parrot".

Prison Dog

The dog that holds the keys to Fort Charles' prison cells is smarter than your average canine, or so it would seem. No one is sure how but he freed Pintel and Ragetti and made a valiant stand against the Pelegostos tribe to help Jack Sparrow escape.

If you're a pirate with a problem you could do worse than pay a visit to this powerful mystic.

Name: Tia Dalma

Rank: Voodoo priestess

Personality: Mysterious, bewitching and eccentric

Skills: Psychic powers, fortune-telling

Weapons: Her knowledge of the sea, her witty charm

Notes of interest: Jack Sparrow and Tia Dalma have been friends for a long time

Gypsy Queen

Tia Dalma has a powerful relationship with the sea. With her psychic mind, she can look deep into a person's soul the first time she meets them. Some take the things she tells them with a pinch of salt, but they do so at their own risk, for this mystic's powers should not be underestimated.

Tia lives in a wooden shack, on the misty banks of the Pantano River. Few pirates like to enter this eerie place unless it's absolutely necessary.

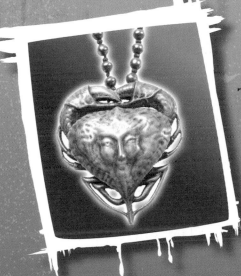

Tia's shack is crammed with strange, mystical objects, including a locket in the shape of a heart, held in a crab's grasp.

Tia's collection of crab claws allows her to see what ordinary folk cannot. By throwing them on a table she was able to tell Jack Sparrow the exact location of Davy Jones' ship.

Tia Dalma

❝ What ... service ... may I do **you?** Hmm? You know I **demand payment.❞**
– *Tia Dalma*

Captain Jack's

Not all objects of value are made from silver or gold. Every pirate possession tells a story and Jack Sparrow's treasured objects are no exceptions.

Magic Compass

Jack's compass points to whatever the person holding it wants most. Trouble is, Jack doesn't always know what he wants most!

Jack's Hat

Jack feels lost without his hat. He was happy then when the Kraken spat it out at him, just moments before it dragged him down to Davy Jones' Locker.

Jar of Dirt

This was given to Jack by Tia Dalma. She told him to keep it with him at all times so he'd always be near land – and safe from Davy Jones!

Treasures

Piece of Eight

Jack wears his Piece of Eight draped over his red bandana. It marks him as one of the nine Pirate Lords.

Jack's Charms

Over the years, Jack has collected many unusual charms and beads, which he likes to tie into his dreadlocked hair.

Hidden Objects

How many times can you find the word "compass" in the grid? The word can read up, down, left or right, but not diagonally. The first one has been done for you.

P	M	O	C	M	C	D	S	C
A	O	S	S	Z	N	P	S	O
S	M	P	A	I	G	H	T	M
S	O	D	C	E	S	S	A	P
P	C	M	O	F	L	D	O	C
S	C	P	R	O	S	S	M	J
S	O	A	S	E	A	E	P	A
S	M	G	S	C	P	F	Z	S
A	P	P	I	E	M	O	C	S

One of Jack's other treasures can be found somewhere in the grid. Clue: Jack wears this item draped over his bandana.

The answer can be found on page 69.

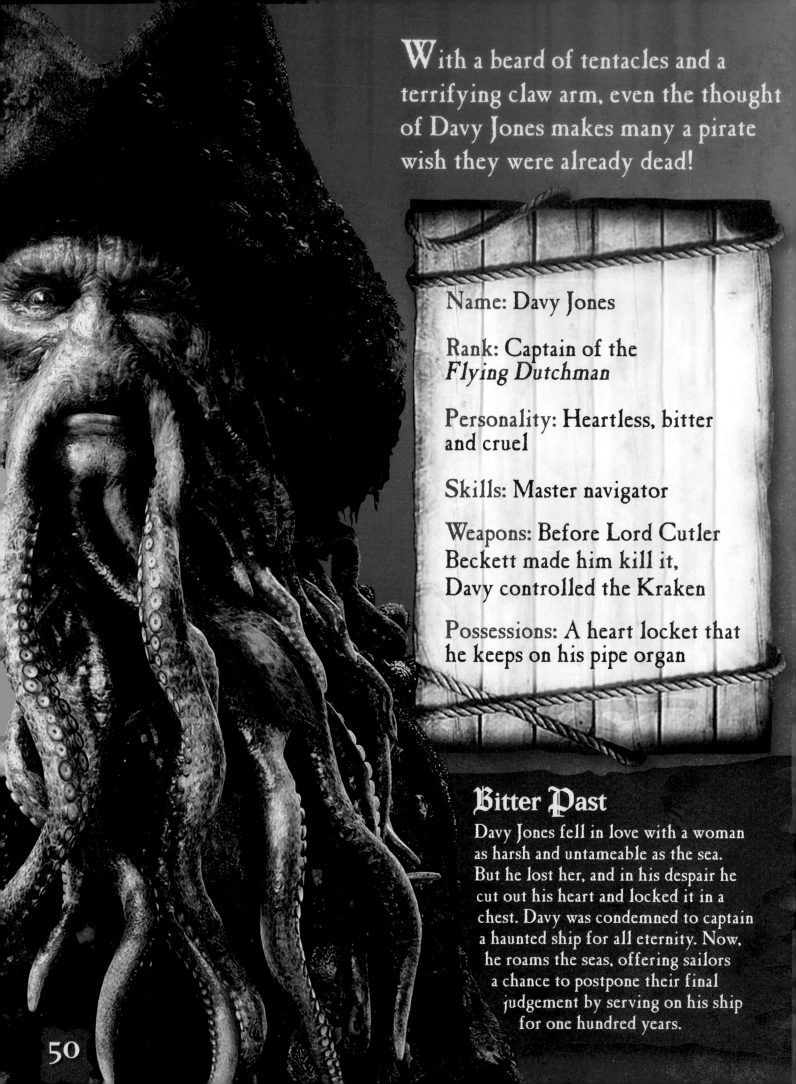

With a beard of tentacles and a terrifying claw arm, even the thought of Davy Jones makes many a pirate wish they were already dead!

Name: Davy Jones

Rank: Captain of the *Flying Dutchman*

Personality: Heartless, bitter and cruel

Skills: Master navigator

Weapons: Before Lord Cutler Beckett made him kill it, Davy controlled the Kraken

Possessions: A heart locket that he keeps on his pipe organ

Bitter Past

Davy Jones fell in love with a woman as harsh and untameable as the sea. But he lost her, and in his despair he cut out his heart and locked it in a chest. Davy was condemned to captain a haunted ship for all eternity. Now, he roams the seas, offering sailors a chance to postpone their final judgement by serving on his ship for one hundred years.

Davy Jones puffs on a pipe made from whalebone. He blows out the smoke through holes in the side of his face.

Davy raised the *Black Pearl* from the ocean floor. In return, after thirteen years, he was owed Jack Sparrow's soul and servitude.

Whoever controls Davy Jones' heart controls the sea. Now in Lord Beckett's possession, Davy has no choice but to serve the East India Trading company.

Davy Jones

" Life is cruel. Why should the **afterlife** be any different?**"**

— *Davy Jones*

Isla

On this deserted island littered with gravestones, it's every man for himself ...

Fight for the Prize

Desperate to affect the outcome of their fates, Jack, Norrington and Will each had their own reasons for wanting Davy's chest and its contents.

Jack needed the chest so he could make a deal with Davy Jones. Otherwise, he would have to serve one hundred years on Davy's ship.

Who do you think was the most desperate to own the contents of the chest?

Norrington saw the promise of redemption in the chest. If he could deliver it to Lord Cutler Beckett of the East India Trading company, his honour would be restored.

Will wanted the chest so he could free his father from his fate aboard the *Flying Dutchman*. Will made a promise to his father that he'd use the knife he gave him to stab Davy Jones' heart – a promise he's determined to keep.

Cruces

Key Chase

The frantic swordfight that took place on Isla Cruces was not for the fainthearted, but Jack, Will and Norrington were all experienced with a sword. Here are some swordfighting tips in case you ever find yourself battling for a key aboard a rolling waterwheel!

Swordfighting Tips

Learn how to move well. Footwork is the basis for a strong attack and a solid defence.

Practise using a sword with both your right and left hands. Being able to swap your sword from hand to hand will unsettle an opponent.

Follow your opponent's eyes. They will tell you all you need to know about his next move.

With Davy Jones' heart in his possession, Lord Cutler Beckett and the East India Trading company's power is growing ... fast!

Name: Lord Cutler Beckett

Personality: Greedy and scheming, will use any means necessary to get what he wants

Skills: Business-minded, very persuasive

Ships: Cutler Beckett has many ships under his command, including his personal ship, the *Endeavour*

Prized possessions: Pirate branding cane, map of the world, Davy Jones' beating heart

Beckett's Master Plan

Lord Cutler Beckett works as a senior officer for the East India Trading Company. This powerful corporation controls much of the Far East's trade and plans to control the West's, too. To help the company achieve its goals, Beckett is determined to stamp out piracy for good.

Beckett keeps a large map in his office that is constantly being redrawn as new islands and countries are discovered.

Some years ago, Beckett used a hot branding cane to leave a "P" scar on Jack Sparrow, marking him forever as a pirate.

Beckett uses an assistant to spy on pirates for him – a mean-spirited man called Mr Mercer.

66 Every man has his price he will willingly accept. Even for what he hopes **never to sell."**

– Lord Cutler Beckett

At World's End

1   With Davy Jones' heart in his possession, Lord Cutler Beckett and the East India Trading Company had power over the *Flying Dutchman* and Davy Jones. Under Beckett's command, Davy and his crew were scouring the seas, executing every pirate they came across.

Also under Beckett's command were Admiral James Norrington and Governor Swann. Davy Jones told the Governor how his pet leviathan, the Kraken, had sunk the *Black Pearl*, taking Elizabeth with it.

Governor Swann was devastated. He went to stab Jones' heart but Norrington stopped him. To slay the heart of Davy Jones would be to take Davy's place as the immortal captain of the *Flying Dutchman* – a fate very few would bring on themselves.

2   Davy Jones was wrong about one thing, for in the bustling harbour of Singapore, Elizabeth Swann was still very much alive. Pained by her part in Jack's fate, she'd joined forces with Jack's old enemy, Captain Barbossa. Captain Barbossa had come back from the dead himself, so if anyone could help them bring Jack back from Davy Jones' Locker, it was going to be him.

3 "Your captain is expecting us," said Barbossa to Tai Huang, a lieutenant. Tai Huang took Elizabeth and Barbossa into a steamy, algae-covered bathhouse – the secret hideout of the notorious Pirate Lord, Captain Sao Feng.

Meanwhile, Gibbs, Pintel, Ragetti, Marty and Cotton approached the bathhouse from the water; their heads hidden under coconut shells. As they filed through metal grates into the steam tunnels, Tia Dalma, disguised as an old woman, pushed a squeaking cart to muffle the noise.

4 Barbossa explained to Sao Feng that they needed a ship and a crew. Feng was angry. Earlier that day, someone had broken into his quarters and stolen his maps to World's End. The thief was brought out – it was Will Turner.

"You come into my city, and you betray me?" snapped Feng, angry to see they were working together. Nevertheless, he was curious to know what they wanted from Davy Jones' Locker.

"Jack Sparrow," said Will, and Feng's face darkened.

Barbossa explained that an emergency meeting of the Brethren Court had been called and all Pirate Lords, including Jack, must be present. Sao Feng didn't like Jack Sparrow, but he agreed that the East India Trading Company must be stopped.

5 Suddenly, the bathhouse was stormed by East India Trading Company agents and a fierce battle broke out. In the gunfire, Will took Sao Feng aside. Will's mission was different to Elizabeth's. He wanted to save his father rather than save Jack, and to do it he needed Jack's ship, the *Black Pearl*.

"If you want to cut a deal with Beckett, you want what I offer," Will told Sao Feng. Sao Feng understood and gave him the maps, a boat and a full crew.

6   Aboard an old junk ship named the *Hai Peng*, Will studied the maps to World's End. They were very cryptic, but Barbossa seemed unconcerned.

"You need to be lost to find a place that can't be found," he said.

Tia Dalma came up on deck and sensed Jack was close. Suddenly, Will heard a rumbling sound. They were heading for a waterfall! Soon, they plummeted down and down into nothingness until they reached the shoreline of Davy Jones' Locker, their ship in tatters.

7   In Davy's Locker, Jack Sparrow was miserable. He didn't like being dead. He still had the *Black Pearl*, but it was motionless on the desert sand and there wasn't the slightest breeze. But suddenly, his ship began to move — it was being carried by hundreds of tiny crabs! He looked up and saw his old crew.

8   "How ye be, Jack Sparrow?" said Barbossa, explaining they'd come to rescue him. Jack was shocked to see Barbossa alive, and was still wary of his old enemy.

"Since I possess a ship and you don't, you're the ones in need of rescuing," said Jack.

With two captains, the *Black Pearl* set sail, but it was getting dark. Tia Dalma feared that if they didn't find a way out of Davy Jones' Locker before nightfall, they were doomed to stay there for eternity.

9 In the cabin, Jack studied the maps and uncovered a message: "Up is down". Jack knew what he had to do. He tricked the crew into running from side to side across the deck until, eventually, the ship completely flipped over! Everything was underwater, but, before long, the water fell away and they were back in the land of the living!

10 Captain Jack and Captain Barbossa rowed to land to fetch water. When they returned, Tai Huang, Sao Feng's lieutenant, pointed a pistol at them. The Chinese pirates led them back on to the *Pearl*, where Sao Feng was waiting for them. Feng's ship, the *Empress*, had moored nearby.

"She's not part of the bargain," said Will, seeing that Elizabeth had been taken captive by Feng's men. "Release her."

"You heard Captain Turner," said Sao Feng. Barbossa and Jack couldn't believe their ears – Captain Turner!

"I'm sorry, Jack," said Feng, catching Jack's arm, "but there's an old friend who wants to see you."

11 Jack was taken to Lord Beckett's cabin on his ship, the *Endeavour*. Picking up Jack's compass, Beckett offered him a job as a privateer. But Jack had a counter-proposal – if Beckett cancelled Jack's debt to Davy, Jack would lead Beckett to the Brethren Court meeting and draw out all the world's most wanted pirates for him.

Back on the *Pearl*, Feng shackled Will, turning on him. Will was furious.

"Beckett agreed the *Black Pearl* was to be mine," said Feng, turning to Beckett's assistant, Mr Mercer. But Feng had also been betrayed.

"Lord Beckett wouldn't give up the one ship as might prove a match for the *Dutchman*, would he?" smiled Mr Mercer.

12   Sao Feng felt they'd have no chance of defeating Beckett's men, but Barbossa was more hopeful.

"We have Calypso," he said. Feng looked at Elizabeth and believed that she must be Calypso – the goddess of the sea trapped in human form. Feng offered to help the *Black Pearl*'s crew defeat Beckett's army, but only if he could keep Elizabeth.

"Done," said Elizabeth, agreeing to the deal.

Soon, Beckett's ship was under attack. The *Empress* was getting away. Seeing his chance to escape, Jack tied himself to a cannon and fired it at the *Pearl*. Sending Will to the brig, he was soon back where he should be – behind the helm of his ship.

13   Aboard the *Empress*, Elizabeth was given a fine Chinese gown to wear. She hadn't expected to be treated so well.

"No other treatment would be worthy of you ... Calypso," said Feng, admiring Elizabeth. Elizabeth didn't understand what he meant, but she decided to keep quiet.

Suddenly, the *Empress* was attacked. The *Dutchman* had found them and sent rounds of cannonfire into the ship's hull. Elizabeth turned and saw Sao Feng had been badly hurt.

14   Feng took off the rope-knot pendant that he wore around his neck.

"The Captain's knot. Take it. Take it!" he urged Elizabeth. "Go in my place to Shipwreck Cove."

Elizabeth held the pendant as lieutenant Tai Huang entered.

"He made me Captain," she said, still not quite believing it.

15 Boarding the *Empress*, Norrington was surprised to see Elizabeth alive, but even more surprised to learn that she was the captain of a Chinese pirate ship. He ordered the *Dutchman* to tow the *Empress* and he led Elizabeth and her crew to the *Dutchman's* brig.

In the brig, Elizabeth met Bootstrap Bill Turner. He'd become almost part of the ship and his mind was failing him. Seeing Bootstrap suffer such a terrible fate helped Elizabeth understand why Will was so desperate to save him.

16 On the *Pearl*, Will Turner had escaped the brig and was leaving a trail of barrels for Beckett.

"What do you intend to do, when you've given up the location of the Brethren?" asked Jack, figuring out Will's plan.

"Ask Beckett to free my father," said Will.

Jack knew Beckett would never risk killing Davy. But Jack had an idea. What if he stabbed Davy's heart? Will's father would still go free and Jack would become the immortal captain of the *Dutchman* and never have to face death again. This plan suited Will, but he was reluctant to trust Jack. Jack gave Will his compass, then pushed him into the sea, with only a barrel to cling to.

17 That night, Admiral Norrington secretly freed Elizabeth and her crew from the *Dutchman's* brig. He told them to scale the tow rope back to the *Empress*. Touched that he'd helped her, Elizabeth urged Norrington to escape with them, but Bootstrap, in his confused state, saw people were escaping and raised the alarm.

"Go!" shouted Norrington.

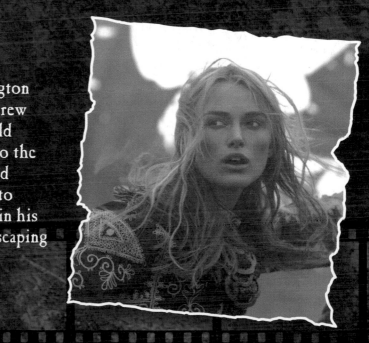

18 Only pirates knew the way into the hollow island that was Shipwreck Cove. In one of the many shipwrecks, the meeting of the Brethren Court was about to begin. Barbossa ordered each Pirate Lord to put his Piece of Eight into a wooden bowl. One by one they did so, apart from Jack. They were still short of one Pirate Lord, so he was happy to wait for Sao Feng.

"Sao Feng is not coming," said Elizabeth, arriving at the meeting and taking Feng's place at the table.

"Listen to me!" she yelled. "Our location has been betrayed. Jones, under the command of Lord Beckett – they are on their way here!"

19 All nine Pirate Lords argued over the options available to them – hide, release Calypso and risk the wrath of the sea, or fight. Jack agreed with Elizabeth that the best idea was to fight.

Barbossa instructed Pintel and Ragetti to gather the Pieces of Eight. Soon, one by one, pirate ships sailed out of the cove; the pirates on board sharpening their swords in preparation. But the pirates' boldness was short-lived, as they saw the entire fleet of the East India Trading Company coming for them.

"Parlay?" suggested Jack.

20 On opposite ends of a sparkling white sand bar, two longboats had beached. From one end walked Jack, Elizabeth and Barbossa. From the other end came Jones, Beckett and Will, who had been found by the *Endeavour*.

This was no ordinary Parlay – this was the pirates against the East India Trading Company.

21 "You be the cur that led these wolves to our door," hissed Barbossa at Will. Beckett laughed this off, explaining how Will was just a tool and that Jack was the real betrayer. After all, if Will was acting alone, how come Beckett had come to own Jack's compass?

22 Slowly, Elizabeth realised what Jack and Will were planning – Jack was going to stab Davy's heart and take his place as the immortal captain.

"There's no better end for Jack Sparrow than bilge rat aboard the *Flying Dutchman*," she said, thinking quickly. She proposed that Will left with them and they could have Jack. Beckett agreed.

As Jack and Will were traded, Jack dropped his Piece of Eight and Barbossa took it. Jack was dragged to the *Flying Dutchman* and the others returned to the *Black Pearl*. The battle of the seas was about to begin.

23 With all nine Pieces of Eight in his possession, Barbossa said the incantation and released Calypso. She rose up and then disappeared just as quickly. They had no idea whether she planned to help or hinder them but it was their only chance. Elizabeth took control of the *Pearl* and ordered the crew to hoist the colours. She was nervous, but she was a Pirate Lord now and had to show her nerve.

Elizabeth drew her sword and led the pirates into the battle of their lives.

"Today ..." she cried, "we are the Pirates of the Caribbean!"

Few pirates from the exotic waters of the Far East are as fearsome as Captain Sao Feng.

Name: Captain Sao Feng

Personality: Mysterious, quiet and brooding

Skills: Stamping his authority on his men, ruthless fighter

Ships: *Empress*

Prized possessions: His unusual rope-knot pendant

Notes of interest: Captain Sao Feng is not a fan of Jack Sparrow

Far East Empire

There are many pirates in the Far East, but Captain Sao Feng is one of the most famous. He keeps guards around his bathhouse at all times. Each guard wears a dragon tattoo, Sao Feng's symbol. For reasons unknown, Sao Feng bears a grudge against Jack Sparrow.

Sao Feng's base is a steamy bathhouse in bustling Singapore.

Sao Feng believed Elizabeth was Calypso, the goddess of the sea trapped in human form.

Feng gave Elizabeth his rope-knot pendant and made her the Captain of the *Empress* – and a Pirate Lord.

" The only reason I would want **Jack Sparrow** returned from the realm of the dead is so I can send him back **myself. "**

– *Sao Feng*

Could You

Have you got what it takes to become a famous pirate? Try this swashbucklin' quiz to find out! Circle a, b or c for each question.

Remember, all the answers can be found somewhere in your Annual. If you get stuck, get searchin'!

1

Which pirate island was named by the Spanish owing to its turtle-like shape?

a) Porta Tortou
b) Tortuga
c) Totorro

2

What did Elizabeth say her surname was when she first met Captain Barbossa?

a) Swann
b) Sparrow
c) Turner

3

What is the pirate word for someone not used to being at sea?

a) landgoer
b) sealubber
c) landlubber

4

Who was Barbossa's undead monkey named after?

a) Bootstrap Bill
b) Jack Sparrow
c) Davy Jones

5

What is the skull and crossbones flag otherwise known as?

a) Jolly Red
b) Jolly Roger
c) Jolly Rhubarb

6

What word must you shout if you want to gain protection from a pirate attack?

a) "Parlay!"
b) "Poorly!"
c) "Poulet!"

7

Which former naval officer-turned-pirate told Elizabeth pirate tales when she was a girl?

a) Cotton
b) Marty
c) Gibbs

Be a Pirate?

8 Who made James Norrington's ceremonial sword?

a) Governor Swann
b) Cutler Beckett
c) Will Turner

9 What is the name of Lord Beckett's assistant?

a) Mullroy
b) Murgatroyd
c) Mercer

10 What did Bootstrap Bill give Will when Will escaped the Flying Dutchman?

a) a knife
b) a map
c) a cutlass

11 Who first had the maps to World's End?

a) Tia Dalma
b) Sao Feng
c) Jack Sparrow

12 What type of building was Sao Feng's hideout?

a) Wooden shack
b) Boathouse
c) Bathhouse

13 Who did Sao Feng give his rope-knot pendant to?

a) Elizabeth Swann
b) Tai Huang
c) Captain Barbossa

14 Where was the meeting of the Pirate Lords held?

a) Shipwreck Cave
b) Shipwreck Harbour
c) Shipwreck Cove

15 Who is often seen smoking a pipe made from whalebone?

a) Jack Sparrow
b) Davy Jones
c) Governor Swann

Now check the answers on page 69 to see how you scored!

The End of Piracy?

The battle to control the Seven Seas is about to begin. It's time to decide whose side you're on ...

The East India Trading Company

Head: Lord Cutler Beckett

Allies: Mercer, Admiral Norrington, Governor Swann and the British Navy

Assets: Wealth, the support of the Crown

Ships: An entire fleet, including the *Endeavour* and the *Flying Dutchman*

Control: Trade throughout the Far East and increasingly in the Carribbean and beyond

Versus ...

The Pirates

Head: The Nine Pirate Lords

Allies: William Turner, Tia Dalma and all the pirate deckhands across the Seven Seas

Assets: Calypso, the goddess of the sea

Ships: The *Black Pearl*

Control: Pirates rule the seas – for now

Who do you think will win the battle?

Answers

p28
Know Your Knots

granny
knot

reef
knot

p66
Could You Be a Pirate?

Award yourself one point for every correct answer, then check your score rating below.

1) b; 2) c; 3) c; 4) b; 5) b; 6) a; 7) c; 8) c;
9) c; 10) a; 11) b; 12) c; 13) a; 14) c; 15) b.

Pirate Score

0-5 points
Hmm. Even Pintel and Ragetti could do better than this!

6-10 points
Not bad. You're definitely no landlubber, that's for sure.

11-15 points
Excellent! You seem suspiciously like a Pirate Lord. Are you sure your name isn't Jack Sparrow?

p44
Jack the Chief

p49
Hidden Objects

The word "compass" appears seven times in the grid, including the one done for you. The mystery treasure is "Piece of Eight".

P	M	O	C	M	C	D	S	C
A	O	S	S	Z	N	P	S	O
S	M	P	A	I	G	H	T	M
S	O	D	C	E	S	S	A	P
P	C	M	O	F	L	D	O	C
S	C	P	R	O	S	S	M	J
S	O	A	S	E	A	E	P	A
S	M	G	S	C	P	F	Z	S
A	P	P	I	E	M	O	C	S